Books by Ian Schrauth

The Opportunity
The Short-Lived social media biz of Darlene Hoffman

A Heart of Fate and Love
Call me maybe: Vol. 1
Faithful: Vol. 1
Faithful: Vol. 2
'Till I find you

270
Behind the Pages

SLMPD

The American Way
Beyond the Veil
Scandalous
Trace My Steps
Within the Air

SLMPD

IAN
SCHRAUTH

Dark Cry Press

HeartStone Virtual Solutions

*To James Patterson & Marshall Karp
the authors who convinced me to write this
thriller.*

PREFACE

As she straightened out her skirt and checked her makeup in the rear view mirror, the woman took a deep breath before shutting off the car engine.

She entered a small conference room at the Aviator Hotel and Suites where an Amway business briefing was being held. Folding chairs were scattered around, and a projector screen dominated one wall.

Opting for a seat towards the back of the room, she observed the diverse group of attendees, each one brimming with anticipation to learn about the opportunities presented by an Amway Independent Business Owner. Or "IBO" for short.

But amidst their enthusiasm, she harbored a different motive.

As the presentation commenced, the woman found herself getting swept away by the speaker's captivating words. The promise of financial freedom, the allure of being her own boss, and the potential for unlimited income seemed almost too good to be true.

***

After the presentation concluded, attendees were encouraged to mingle and engage with the distributors present. The woman meandered through the room, sipping on her complimentary soda and striking up conversations with various distributors.

As the night wore on and the crowd began to thin out, the woman noticed a middle-aged woman distributor packing up her materials. Intrigued, she decided to discreetly follow her out to the parking lot.

Dressed in a suit and clutching a large binder filled with papers, the distributor appeared taken aback but swiftly regained her composure as the woman approached. They engaged in conversation about the business, and the woman listened intently, nodding along to the distributor's words. She couldn't help but notice how well the distributor seemed to know her and her interests — it was as if he had done his research beforehand.

During their conversation, the distributor pulled out a pamphlet and handed it to the woman, urging her to attend another meeting. Curiosity piqued, she glanced at the pamphlet while the distributor made her way to the car and drove off. The woman decided to follow suit, tailing the distributor's car.

***

When the distributor got home, she walked into his apartment and sat her fake Rolex watch on the counter.

She walked into the bathroom and stared to get undressed to get in the shower.

While she was getting undressed, the lady was following her close by, without her knowledge. She snuck into her apartment, grabbed her fake Rolex watch, and waited for her to turn on the shower.

After the shower was turned on, she pulled out her revolver and headed to the bathroom where the distributor was at.

As she quietly opened the door, she was washing her hair in the shower. She seemed at peace.

As she put his her under the water, she pulled the trigger at his head.

Her body tumbled down as the lady rushed out.

PART ONE

CHAPTER 1

I groggily reached out to hit the snooze button on my alarm, wanting to go back to sleep.

"Ugh, do I HAVE to get up?" I thought while I stared at the white, popcorn celling.

Although my tired body *wanted* to sleep, the realization that I am an adult and have a "big boy job" sat with me and jolted me awake.

Reluctantly, I dragged myself out of bed, hastily donned my police jacket, snatched my police gear from the safe on my nightstand, and headed out.

Stepping out into the early morning light, I inhaled the crisp air, tinged with a hint of anticipation.

St. Louis wore its own unique charm despite its flaws—the iconic arch, the soulful Blues, and the unforgettable St. Louis-style Chinese food—giving me a sense of belonging.

I had no desire to move to another city to do detective work for their police presents. Not San Francisco, no New York, not even Bubblefuck, Alaska.

I hoped into my car, and started to drive down Highway 50.

At a red light, I turned on a morning show by a political candidate I follow named Austin Peterson, and listened to what he had to say about the lates nationwide political gossip taking place.

***

Arriving at the station, I made my way up to my shared office where my partner-in-solving-crimes, Kendall Marie, was already engrossed in files.

She glanced up, nodding in acknowledgment. "Morning, RJ."

"Morning, Kendall," I replied, stifling a yawn. "What's on our plate today?"

Handing me a file, Kendall's expression turned serious. "Murder at an Amway business briefing," she said, her words raising my eyebrows in surprise.

At the Aviator...I see....

"It's an unusual one. The victim is a young woman, Sarah Johnson. We don't have much to go on, but Lieutenant Petras want us on the case."

A surge of excitement coursed through me. It had been a slow few week, and the prospect of a challenging investigation was invigorating.

"Let's dive in," I stated.

We gathered additional materials and briefings, studying the limited information at our disposal.

Sarah Johnson, a 23-year-old, had been attending an Amway business briefing in South St. Louis when she was found dead in the bathroom, a single gunshot hole to her head.

No weapon or fingerprints were discovered at the scene.

The show is only getting started...

***

As Kendall drove us to the crime scene, we engaged in a detailed discussion, exploring various possibilities.

Our conversation went through potential motives:

Was it a targeted attack or a random act of violence?

Did Sarah have any connections that could have led to her demise?

Arriving at the crime scene — a small apartment now swathed in police tape — we observed the flurry of activity. Police examined the surroundings for any overlooked clues while forensics handled the apartment.

Kendall and I got on gloves and stepped inside the apartment. The air hung heavy with death.

The bathroom door beckoned, its secrets waiting to be unraveled.

Pushing open the door, we surveyed the small, cramped space. I crouched near the lifeless body of Sarah Johnson, taking in the sight before me.

Her once vibrant existence reduced to stillness, her dreams forever silenced.

I couldn't help but feel a feeling of empathy for the young woman whose life had been abruptly cut short.

As we meticulously combed the crime scene, we documented every detail, no matter how seemingly insignificant. Photographs captured the room from multiple angles, preserving the evidence for analysis. Each item collected held the potential to provide a breakthrough—the smallest thread leading to the truth.

Leaving the apartment, Kendall and I reconvened in the car, our minds buzzing with fragments of the investigation.

We exchanged our initial theories, considering the motive behind the murder.

"Was Sarah's killing a tragic consequence of being in the "wrong place at the wrong time"?" She asked.

"Or it could be a targeted effort." I replied, backing out of the parking space. "We need to know if she had any enemies. Maybe she had someone that was envious of her and wanted her dead."

"She got murdered at a hotel at something called a "business breefing." She stated and pulled out her phone.

Kendall typed a few things on the screen and pulled up something. "According to Reddit, which we all know is a *very reliable* source, an Amway business briefing is where they try and recruit new people as...what sounds like Amway Sales representative."

"Like recruiting people into a cult?" I asked.

"Kind of like that."

CHAPTER 2

Kendall and I sat silently in the car after going through theories, driving back to the station.

The silence is palpable, the weight of the case heavy on our minds. We're both lost in thought, trying to process the little information we have.

The streets of St. Louis are bustling with morning traffic, but I'm barely paying attention.

I keep thinking about Sarah.

Who was she?

What led her to that Amway meeting in the first place?

And most importantly, who killed her?

I try to push those thoughts aside as we arrive at the station. Kendall and I head back up to our office, where we immediately get to work.

We start poring over the evidence we've gathered so far, trying to piece together a timeline of events.

I can't help but feel frustrated. We've got a few shell casings and a stray hair, but nothing that points us in the direction of a suspect. It's like we're grasping at straws.

Kendall is cool-headed and methodical, and I know she won't let us get bogged down in frustration.

How do I know this? We've been working as partners in the SLMPD for about two years. We then were promoted from being regular cops, to being part of the Major Case Team, sometimes coined as "Team Gateway".

Since St. Louis' Reform Party mayor Jill Johnson created this team as a campaign promise four months ago, it's been going very strong.

And I have to say this about Jill: For a mayor that's a part of a third-party, it's going *amazing*!

Kendall was on the phone, trying to track down any leads on Sarah Johnson.

I start digging through the files, trying to find anything that might give us a clue.

As I sift through the papers, I catch a whiff of Kendall's coffee. It's a small thing, but it reminds me that there's still some normalcy in the world. We may be working a murder case, but life goes on.

My eyes start to blur as I read through page after page of reports, but I force myself to keep going. We need to find a lead, a piece of evidence, anything that will give us a break in the case.

As I'm reading, Kendall looks up from her computer. "Hey, RJ, I found something."

I immediately sit up straighter, eager for any information. "What is it?"

"Sarah Johnson was a graduate student at St. Louis University," Kendall says. "She was studying marketing and had been interning at a local advertising agency. Her coworkers say she was smart and hardworking, but didn't have many friends outside of work."

I start to feel a flicker of hope. Maybe this is a lead we can follow up on. "What about her family?"

"They live in Jefferson County now," Kendall replies. "I'm trying to get in touch with them now."

CHAPTER 3

As Kendall continues her attempts to reach Sarah's family, I decide to dig deeper into Sarah's background.

I search through social media platforms, looking for any clues or connections that might shed light on her life.

Scrolling through her profiles, I notice that she had recently posted about attending a seminar on personal growth and success. The timing lines up with the Amway meeting.

I turn to Kendall, who has managed to reach Sarah's parents. "They're on their way here," she informs me, her voice tinged with a mix of empathy and urgency. "They should be here shortly."

I take a deep breath and stand up from my desk. "Let's meet them in the conference room.

Maybe they can give us some insight into Sarah's recent activities."

***

Once we got the notification that they arrived, we make our way to the conference room. As we enter, I notice the pain etched on the faces of Sarah's parents. They look devastated, their eyes red from crying.

"Mr. and Mrs. Johnson, I'm Detective RJ, and this is my partner, Kendall," I introduce us with a sympathetic tone. "We're investigating the unfortunate circumstances surrounding Sarah's death, and we're hoping you can help us understand what she was involved in recently."

Mr. Johnson, a middle-aged man with weary eyes, clears his throat and begins to speak. "Sarah had been struggling with some personal issues lately. She seemed restless, searching for something more in life. She had mentioned attending a seminar on personal growth, but we didn't think much of it."

Mrs. Johnson, a fragile-looking woman, adds, "She had always been ambitious, trying to find her way in the world. We supported her dreams, but we were worried about her becoming too trusting of people. She was always looking for that breakthrough."

"Do you know which seminar she attended?" Kendall asks, her voice gentle but inquisitive.

Mr. Johnson furrows his brow, deep in thought. "I can't recall the name, but she did mention something about a company called Amway. She said she met some interesting people there who talked about financial independence and success."

Kendall and I exchange glances, realizing that this new piece of information aligns with what we had discovered at the crime scene.

"I believe Sarah attended an Amway meeting shortly before her death," I say, trying to choose my words carefully. "Do you know anyone she might have mentioned or anything that could connect her to this group?"

Mr. Johnson shakes his head, his voice filled with regret. "I wish I could help you more, but Sarah was becoming more distant. She was keeping things to herself, and we didn't pry too much."

Mrs. Johnson wipes away a tear, her voice quivering. "Please find out what happened to our daughter. She deserved *so* much more."

Kendall and I exchange a determined look, silently vowing to bring justice to Sarah's memory.

"We'll do everything we can," I assure them, my tone resolute.

CHAPTER 4

Relieved to have completed my work for the day, I step out of the station and take in a deep breath of fresh air.

The weight of the case momentarily lifted; I find myself contemplating how to spend my evening.

A pang of hunger reminds me of my neglected stomach, prompting me to make my way to the familiar comfort of my favorite bar — a place where I can unwind and satiate my appetite.

Entering the dimly lit establishment, I find solace in the familiar ambiance.

Taking a seat at the counter, I prepare to order my usual beer. However, my attention is abruptly diverted by the presence of a captivating woman a few seats away. Her azure eyes and cascading curls command attention, and she seems deeply engrossed in the contents of her phone.

Summoning a surge of courage, I approach her with a friendly smile. "Hey, I'm RJ. Mind if I join you?"

She glances up from her phone, returning the smile and nodding graciously. "Sure, I'm Rachel."

Engaging in conversation, I discover that Rachel is a sales representative for a Multi-Level marketing (MLM) company called Monat.

Initially, I had mistaken her for an Amway sales representative, only to remember the striking similarities shared by these MLM entities from researching my case. Despite my reservations, Rachel's infectious enthusiasm draws me in, making it hard to resist her charm.

As we place our food orders, Rachel takes the opportunity to elaborate on the Monat business model.

Deep down, I am aware of the controversies surrounding these legal pyramid schemes and their questionable practices.

So, how large is your team?" I asked.

"Currently, I have around 50 people on my team," Rachel responds. "But I'm always on the lookout for new individuals to join us."

I nod thoughtfully. "Impressive. How long have you been involved with this?"

She hesitates for a moment before answering, raising a small flicker of doubt within me. "About a year and a half now. I've seen incredible results. I've even been able to quit my full-time job and enjoy the freedom of working from home."

A smile forms on my lips, but skepticism lingers in the back of my mind. "So, would you say most of your income comes from recruiting new members, or from product sales?"

Rachel takes a sip of her drink, contemplating her response. "Honestly, it's a mix of both. However, I place great emphasis on fostering genuine relationships with my customers and team members. Building trust ensures their continued loyalty and support."

I could tell her statement on income was a lie...

I absorb her words, silently mulling over the information shared.

As we conclude our meals, Rachel extends an invitation for me to attend a Monat event with her next week.

My instinctive response is a resounding refusal.

Politely settling the bill, we bid each other farewell, and I watch her depart, leaving behind a trail of unanswered questions and a hint of caution from my gut.

CHAPTER 5

The woman observed the room as she settled into her seat. The venue was a lavish hotel ballroom, adorned with glimmering chandeliers and opulent decorations. The atmosphere was buzzing with excitement and anticipation as more people filtered into the room.

She couldn't help but feel a surge of exhilaration, knowing that amidst this crowd, she could find her next victim.

The thought sent a shiver down her spine, a twisted thrill that fueled her dark desires.

As the room at the gym at St. Louis Community College filled with eager attendees, Lauren, the charismatic master distributor for Amway, took the stage.

Her sparkling smile and persuasive charm captivated the room, ensuring that all eyes were on her.

The woman watched intently, analyzing Lauren's every move and word, seeking vulnerabilities that she could exploit.

Lauren began her presentation, introducing the company's revolutionary products, highlighting success stories, and emphasizing the financial opportunities available to those who joined.

She showcased the extravagant lifestyle she claimed to have achieved through her new MLM endeavors, enticing the crowd with promises of wealth and freedom.

The woman played her part effortlessly, nodding and applauding at the appropriate moments, blending seamlessly into the crowd. She engaged in small talk with the individuals seated next to her, expertly concealing her true intentions beneath a facade of friendliness and enthusiasm.

As the event progressed, the woman's eyes scanned the room, searching for her ideal target. She assessed each attendee, evaluating their vulnerabilities and potential for exploitation. She noted the ones who seemed desperate for a change in their lives, those who appeared financially strained, or those whose trust could easily be won.

Finally, her gaze fell upon a middle-aged woman sitting alone at a nearby table.

The woman's weary expression hinted at a difficult life, and her eyes revealed a glimmer of hope mixed with apprehension. Something about her vulnerability called out to the nameless woman, who saw an opportunity to manipulate and control.

As Lauren's presentation reached its climax, the room erupted into applause.

The woman joined in, clapping with fervor, while her mind buzzed with anticipation.

This is the one...

CHAPTER 6

When the reception came to an end, there weren't that many people talking to each other, like at the Amway business briefing.

The woman offered to help clean up the gym in preparation for the next school day, and started to talk with Lauren.

"So, how did you get started in Network marketing?" Lauren asked. "And are you looking at adding another income source to your portfolio as a business owner?"

"I got started a while ago when I was introduced to Amway." The woman replied, putting the last chair on the storage area. "I might be interested. Can I have your number?"

Lauren gave the woman a business card as they walked out to the parking lot.

"Thank you *so* much for this!" The woman exclaimed. "I will *Definity be in touch.*"

"Well, I'm headed to the Popeyes near my apartment. Wanna join me?"

"No thank you." The woman replied.

As Lauren got into her car, the woman watched her as she pulled out of the parking lot.

The woman checked her glove compartment to see if her "special toy" was in there, and after checking, she followed her.

***

The woman observed the middle-aged woman's car as it pulled into the Popeyes parking lot.

The evening darkness provided cover for her intentions.

She parked her own vehicle discreetly to the side of the fast-food restaurant, positioning herself strategically to maintain visual contact with her target.

With a subtle motion, the woman reached into her glove compartment, retrieving a sleek, silenced handgun.

She felt the cold steel against her palm, its weight familiar and comforting. Steadying her nerves, she focused on the task at hand, her determination unwavering.

Inside the middle-aged woman's car, a mixture of anticipation and curiosity filled the air. She had hoped for a quick bite to eat, a respite from the long day she had just endured.

Her window lowered, allowing the evening breeze to graze her face as she scanned the menu displayed on the illuminated board.

But instead of the comforting sound of a voice emanating from the drive-through speaker, the middle-aged woman was met with an eerie silence.

Confusion clouded her expression as she leaned closer to the speaker, calling out with a hint of frustration, "Hello? Is anyone there?"

Unbeknownst to her, the woman outside had taken aim through the darkness.

Her finger tightened around the trigger, and with a deafening crack, a single bullet pierced the stillness of the night.

Time seemed to slow as the middle-aged woman's life was abruptly cut short.

The bullet found its mark, ending her existence with a swift and tragic finality.

The woman watched as her prey slumped forward in her seat, the weight of mortality stealing away her vitality.

CHAPTER 7

I woke up the next morning feeling exhausted. The previous night had been long, and my head was pounding.

I rubbed my eyes and checked my phone.

Ugh…DO I HAVE to get up?

Rubbing my eyes, I reached for my phone, hoping for some reprieve or distraction.

As I scrolled through the notifications, a breaking news alert caught my attention.

The headline sent a chill down my spine: "Mysterious Murder Shocks City: Top Primerica distributor shot in the head in Popeyes Drive through."

My heart skipped a beat as I clicked on the article, my mind racing with thoughts of the previous night's events.

How the fuck did the media get to cover this THAT quickly?!

My next task, a shower, offered a brief respite, the hot water cascading over my weary body, providing temporary relief to the tension in my neck.

However, it did little to alleviate the pounding in my head, which persisted like an unwelcome guest.

I dressed hastily and made my way to the police precinct, knowing that the day ahead would demand my full attention.

**

When I arrived, Kendall was already there. She was hunched over her desk, typing furiously on her computer. "Morning," I said, trying to sound more awake than I felt.

"Good morning, RJ. You look like hell," Kendall said, smirking at me.

"Thanks, I feel like it too," I replied, collapsing into my chair.

"Rough night?"

"I went out with a girl last night, but it didn't go too well," I said, rubbing my temples.

"Uh-oh, what happened?"

"She tried to get me to be a Monat seller with her."

"Eww." She replied. "I'd rather keep my hair from falling out."

True…

As I was about to start on finding some evidence to yesterday's case, Kendall stated, "Lieutenant Petras assigned us a new case."

"Let me guess: it's the one about the murder in the Popeyes drivethrough?" I asked.

"How did you—"

I interrupted. "Saw it on the news this morning.

"Wait, *how* did the news get to it so fast?" She asked.

"Beats me. I was asking the same damn question."

She looked stumped, then said, "Petras isn't gonna like this *one bit*."

"I know."

Kendall and I begin sifting through the evidence we had gathered.

We have a lot of work ahead of us, and it's crucial that we move quickly. We start by reviewing the surveillance footage from the apartment complex where the victim, Laura, was found dead.

It's slow-going at first, but eventually, we spot something that catches our attention.

In the footage, we see what looks like a woman-shaped man dressed in all black slip into the room where the briefing was being held.

They're only in the frame for a few seconds, but it's enough to pique our interest.

We decide to focus our investigation on identifying this person and determining their connection to the victim.

CHAPTER 8

Kendall and I arrived at the apartment complex where Laura lived.

It was a modest building, but well-maintained. We walked up to the front door and rang the bell. A man in his mid-thirties answered the door, looking bleary-eyed and confused.

"SLMPD. Team Gateway. We're investigating the death of one of your neighbors," I said, holding up my badge.

The man nodded and let us in. We asked him a few questions about the night of the murder, but he didn't have much to offer.

We went to the next door, and the next, but everyone said the same thing. No one heard or saw anything out of the ordinary, even with the Popeyes being just across the fence from her complex.

As we knocked on the last door on the third floor, a middle-aged woman answered. She looked familiar.

"Hi, I'm Kendall and this is RJ. We're investigating Laura's death," Kendall said, holding out her badge.

The man's face fell. "Oh, Laura. She was such a sweet girl. I can't believe she's gone."

We asked her if she had any information that could help us.

He shook his head, but then mentioned that Laura used to have people over for meetings. "I don't know any of them, but they were always here. It was always about Amway, selling their products and trying to recruit people."

"Do you have any more information?" I asked.

"Yes. Come in." he said and invited us in.

Kendall and I sat down on the couch as the old man came into the living room.

"Can I offer you guys some tea or cookes?" He asked.

"No thank you. Just here for business." Kendall replied.

"Can you tell us more about Laura's involvement in Amway, Mr…?" I trailed off.

"Kopland. Call me Andrew."

"Thank you, Andrew."

John nodded, taking a sip of his coffee. "Yeah, Laura was one of the top sellers in our district. She was always pushing for more sales and had a lot of people under her in her downline."

"Do you know who her direct downline was?" Kendall asked, leaning forward.

John thought for a moment before answering. "I don't have the exact names, but I can get you in touch with someone who might know more. Laura hosted a lot of meetings in her apartment, and I'm sure some of her downline members were there."

"Thank you. Also, do you know if Laura had any business dealings that went wrong or if anyone had a grudge against her?"

John shook his head. "I'm not aware of anything like that. Laura was always professional and kept things strictly business. But I do know that she had some trouble with a few customers who weren't satisfied with their purchases."

"Interesting," Kendall murmured, jotting down some notes. "Could you give us more details about that?"

John nodded, launching into a story about a disgruntled customer who had threatened to sue Laura over a product that didn't work as advertised.

***

After about an hour of interviewing him, we thanked John and headed out of the complex, something caught my eye. I glanced down and saw a phone lying on the ground near the dumpster. I picked it up and noticed that it was Laura's phone.

Kendall and I exchanged a look and quickly decided to go back into the complex to look for something else. We headed to Laura's apartment and searched through her belongings.

As we searched, we came across a folder with a few printed-out emails.

One of them caught our attention - it was from someone threatening to murder her.

The messages were filtered into spam and it was clear that Laura hadn't seen them

The messages sounded like they were from someone that had a bad business dealing with Laura.

We looked at each other, both thinking the same thing - this could be a lead.

CHAPTER 9

I dialed Rachel's number, hoping to get some more insight into the case. As the phone rang, I could feel the tension building inside me. I needed to find answers, and Rachel was the only lead I had at the moment.

"Hello?" Rachel's voice sounded tired and distracted.

"Hey, it's me, RJ. I wanted to talk to you about the case," I said, trying to sound casual.

"Oh, right. What's up?" she replied, her voice lacking enthusiasm.

"I was thinking about the security footage from the night of the break-in. Do you think it's possible someone tampered with it?" I asked, hoping to spark her interest.

"Yeah, I guess that's possible," she said, but I could tell she wasn't really engaged in the conversation.

"And I was also wondering if you had any suspects in mind," I continued, trying to keep her attention.

Rachel hesitated for a moment before responding, "Not really. I mean, there are some rumors about shady people in the MLM industry, but I don't have any solid ideas."

I could feel my frustration building. It was clear that Rachel wasn't interested in talking about the case. She had her own life and her own problems, and I couldn't blame her for not wanting to get involved.

"Hey, is everything alright?" I asked, sensing that there was something else on her mind.

"Yeah, I'm fine. Just tired," she replied, her voice distant.

I knew I should let her go and not push her to talk about something she didn't want to discuss. "Alright, well, we can talk more about it later if you want," I said, trying to hide my disappointment.

"Yeah, maybe," she mumbled.

Just then, I heard a baby crying in the background. "Is that your baby?" I asked, surprised.

"Yeah, sorry. She's been fussy all day," Rachel replied, sounding a bit exasperated.

"Don't worry about it. Take care of her first," I said, suddenly feeling guilty for bothering her with the case.

"No, it's fine. I'm glad you called. It's just been a long day," Rachel said, her voice softening.

"I understand. Being a parent is tough," I said, trying to be supportive.

"Yeah, it is," Rachel sighed. "Listen, I'm really sorry I can't be more helpful with the case. It's just been a lot to handle lately."

"Don't worry about it," I said, trying to sound reassuring. "We'll figure this out. And if you ever need someone to talk to, I'm here."

"Thanks, RJ. I appreciate that," Rachel said, sounding grateful.

We chatted for a few more minutes about her baby and how she was adjusting to motherhood. I could tell that Rachel was still preoccupied with her own life, but she seemed to appreciate the distraction.

As we said our goodbyes and hung up, I couldn't help but feel a mix of emotions.

On one hand, I understood that Rachel had her own challenges to deal with, and the case wasn't her responsibility.

But on the other hand, I couldn't help but feel frustrated that I couldn't get any valuable information from her.

CHAPTER 10

The woman stepped into the library, the scent of old books filling her senses. It was a peaceful haven, a place she often sought solace in the midst of chaos. As she roamed the aisles, her mind was still preoccupied with the events of the previous day, the chase, and the arrest.

Lost in her thoughts, she nearly collided with a familiar face. It was the lady she recognized from the Amway business briefing she had attended a few months back. They had never spoken before, but the woman couldn't help but feel a strange connection to her.

"Sorry, I wasn't looking where I was going," the woman said, offering a polite smile.

The lady smiled back warmly. "No problem at all. I'm glad we ran into each other. I've been meaning to reach out to you after the briefing, but I never got around to it."

The woman raised an eyebrow, surprised by the unexpected conversation. "Oh, really? I didn't think we had much in common."

The lady chuckled. "You'd be surprised. I remember seeing you at the briefing, and I couldn't help but notice your enthusiasm. You seemed really interested in what they had to say."

The woman nodded, remembering how intrigued she had been by the promises of financial freedom and success. "Yes, I was curious about the MLM business model. It sounded promising, but I haven't really pursued it further."

The lady leaned in, her voice dropping to a conspiratorial whisper. "To be honest, it's not as easy as they make it sound. I joined Amway a few years ago, and while it's been a learning experience, it hasn't been the success story I was hoping for."

Curiosity piqued, the woman leaned in closer, wanting to hear more. "Really? What happened?"

The lady sighed, a hint of disappointment in her eyes. "Well, I invested a lot of time and money into it, but the results just weren't there. It's a tough business, and not everyone succeeds. I realized that it wasn't for me, but I know others who have had better luck."

The woman nodded, grateful for the honesty. "I appreciate you sharing that with me. It's good to know the reality of it all before diving in."

The lady smiled, her warmth putting the woman at ease. "Absolutely. It's important to do your research and make an informed decision. There are so many MLM companies out there, and they all promise the world, but not all of them deliver."

As they continued to chat, the woman found herself opening up about her own struggles and fears. It was a surprising turn of events, but she felt a sense of comfort in confiding in someone who had been through a similar experience.

After a while, the conversation naturally came to an end. The woman watched as her new victim got into her car before getting into hers.

CHAPTER 11

When the lady got home, she opened the front door, and headed into her family room. She put the books she checked out on the counter, and headed to her room to let the dog out of her cage.

As she was heading to her room, the woman quietly entered her house, her gun in her hand.

The woman scurried through the house and noticed she was in her room. She heard a cage unlock, and a dog bark.

"Oh *hello* Bubby! I missed you!" the lady stated.

The woman could hear the lady start to exit her room.

Shit! The woman thought.

The woman rushed into the bathroom next to the room, and hid behind the door. Her heart was pounding because her plans have *never* not gone correctly.

As the woman walked passed the bathroom, not even batting an eye at the now-occupied, dark bathroom, the woman busted out of the bathroom and pulled the trigger to the lady's head.

With the sound of a shockwave, the woman dropped down to the ground leaving Bubby to look at the woman standing in front of her.

I guess you're a bonus to this. She through as she scooped up his little body and rushed out.

CHAPTER 12

The next day, we were fully immersed in our work, sifting through piles of evidence and conducting research.

As our anticipation filled the room, the door to our office swung open with a creak, and the police Lieutenant, Karl Petras, stepped in. His stern expression and graying hair conveyed a sense of authority and experience. His presence alone demanded attention and respect.

Lieutenant Petras glanced around the room, his piercing eyes finally settling on Kendall and me. We straightened up in our chairs, intrigued by the sudden interruption and the prospect of a fresh investigation. It was rare for the Lieutenant himself to deliver a case to us personally.

"Detectives, I have another case for you," he announced, his voice tinged with urgency. The gravity of his words hung in the air, sparking a surge of anticipation within us. "We have a feeling it's linked to your current one."

Kendall and I exchanged glances, our curiosity piqued. We had become accustomed to the monotony of our previous case, and the arrival of a new challenge was a welcome change. Kendall, always brimming with enthusiasm, couldn't contain her excitement as she leaned forward, eager to learn more.

"What's the case, Lieutenant?" she inquired, her tone filled with a mixture of professionalism and genuine intrigue. Her eyes locked onto the folder that Lieutenant Petras was carrying, wondering what secrets it held within its confines.

Lieutenant Petras stepped forward, his hand extending to pass the folder to Kendall. As she accepted it, I caught a glimpse of its contents — photographs, reports, and details neatly organized within its pages. This was a case that required our immediate attention.

"We've got a murder on our hands," Lieutenant Petras began, his voice lowering slightly as he shared the grave news. "The victim's name is Joss Kallaway. But this isn't your ordinary homicide. There's a strong reason to believe it's connected to the one you're currently working on."

Kendall's eyes widened with intrigue, and she turned to me, a glimmer of excitement in her gaze. "Did you hear that, Jake? It seems like we're about to delve even deeper into the rabbit hole."

I nodded in agreement, sharing her enthusiasm for the complex web of connections we were about to unravel. "Looks like our work is far from over. We need to follow this lead and see where it takes us."

Lieutenant Petras, observing our eagerness, nodded approvingly. "That's the spirit, detectives. I have faith in your abilities to piece together the puzzle. This case requires your expertise and attention to detail. Remember, every little clue matters."

As he turned to leave, Kendall couldn't help but ask, "Lieutenant, do we have any leads or suspects in this case? Any particular angle we should focus on?"

Lieutenant Petras paused for a moment, contemplating his response. "At this early stage, we're still gathering information. But I can tell you this much: Joss Kallaway had some ties to the criminal underworld. Keep that in mind as you dig deeper. I have a feeling there's more to this story than meets the eye."

Kendall and I exchanged another glance.

This killer is going to be the end of me...

CHAPTER 13

Kendall and I delved into the contents of the folder, eager to uncover the secrets held within. The photographs and reports painted a vivid picture of Joss Kallaway's life and the circumstances surrounding her tragic demise.

As we scanned through the documents, one detail caught our attention—a mention of Joss Kallaway's involvement as an Amway distributor. The revelation added another layer of complexity to the case, raising questions about potential motives and connections within the Amway network. It was clear that we needed to explore this angle further.

"Joss Kallaway. Another Amway distributor," Kendall mused aloud, her brows furrowing in thought. "Could her murder *really* be connected with the one we're currently working on?"

I shrugged my shoulder, considering the possibility. "It's certainly a lead worth pursuing. Let's dig deeper into her family connections and see if anything stands out."

***

After hours of combed through the internet, meticulously noting down names, addresses, and any other relevant information related to Joss Kallaway's family. We wanted to establish a timeline of her activities, identify potential associates, and gather insights that could lead us closer to the truth.

As we sifted through the records, another detail emerged — the fact that Joss Kallaway was a grandmother to six grandchildren, with two children of her own.

It struck a chord with Kendall and me. The thought of grieving family members seeking justice for their loved one added a personal dimension to our investigation.

"Kendall, let's start by reaching out to Joss Kallaway's child who resides in...Looks like Kentucky," I suggested, realizing the importance of gathering information from family members. "They might be able to shed light on any recent developments in her life or any potential enemies she might have had."

"Do you have her number?"

I looked at the BeenVerified webpage, and read out the number to Kendall.

There was a small pause after I finished so she could finish writing it down.

"She has another son in Oakville. I will go visit him at his workplace."

Kendall nodded, her determination mirroring mine. "I'll make the call right away and see what we can uncover.

I gathered my belongings, preparing for the 5 minute ride to Walmart on Telegraph Road to meet with the other child face-to-face.

CHAPTER 14

I drove along the familiar streets, my mind focused on the upcoming meeting with Joss Kallaway's son.

Although I wanted to help find justice for this case, I did NOT want to enter that WalMart.

Why did he have to work at the worst one in the state?!

As I parked my car in the parking lot, I couldn't help but feel a mixture of anticipation and apprehension.

This conversation had the potential to unveil crucial information that could guide our investigation in unforeseen directions.

Entering the bustling Walmart through the Home and Pharmacy Entrance, I navigated to left and found a manager standing in front of a room with a buhc of employees gathering prepared orders to take out.

It looks like this was the room for deliveries.

"Excuse me, Ma'am." I stated.

"Can I help you?" the woman asked.

"Detective RJ, SLMPD." I introduced and showed my badge.

"We didn't call for you guys." She stated.

"I'm here to see Andrew Kallaway."

She looked confused. "What happened?"

"It's an ongoing investigation regarding his mother, Joss."

She looked shocked, and turned back to the room. "Ethan! Are you taking out that order?"

"Yes. What does it look like I'm doing?" he asked as he headed out the door.

I see I'm dealing with a micromanager...

"Let me call for him." She replied to me, without an apology (or anything) and headed over to the phone. She punched in some numbers and said. "Attention WalMart Associates. Attention Walmart Associates. Ethan from Electronics, please report to the OGP room. Ethan from Electronics, please report to the OGP room." And hung up.

As she was walking back, she paused and picked up a hanging wire from her earpiece. "I have a detective here to see him." She said in the mic and walked back to me. "He'll be here in a moment."

CHAPTER 15

"Excuse me, are you Andrew Kallaway?" I asked as I saw someone walk up.

"Yes, that's me. How can I help you?"

"My name is Detective RD. I'm investigating the murder of your mother, Joss Kallaway. I was hoping we could talk about her and any potential information you might have regarding recent events in her life," I explained, emphasizing the importance of our conversation.

Andrew's expression shifted from curiosity to a mix of sorrow and concern.

"Oh my... I had no idea!"

"You two can go into the side office." The manager stated and directed us to the side office.

She open the door, and saw another employee getting a till from a machine. "Seda, can you step out for a second? I have a detective that needs to talk to Andrew."

"Sure." She replied in a Bosnian accent and walked out

He led me into the office. Andrew gestured for me to take a seat as he closed the door behind us, creating a private space for our discussion.

Taking a moment to compose himself, Andrew settled into his chair, his eyes reflecting a profound sadness. "I can't believe she's gone. It's been such a shock for our family."

"I understand this is a difficult time for you," I offered sympathetically. "But I believe that finding answers and seeking justice can bring some closure. Is there anything you can share about your mother's recent activities or anyone who might have had ill intentions towards her?"

Andrew leaned back in his chair, his gaze fixed on a family photo displayed on his desk. "Mom was a loving grandmother to her six grandchildren. She cherished family and her involvement in Amway. But lately, she had mentioned some tensions within her Amway network. There were rumors of disputes, especially with a fellow distributor named Lisa Thompson."

My interest piqued at the mention of Lisa Thompson. "Can you provide any further details about this Lisa Thompson? Do you know where she resides or have any contact information?"

Andrew pondered for a moment before retrieving his phone from his pocket. "I have her number saved here. Mom used to mention her quite often. She lives a few towns over, in Mehlville. I hope this helps with your investigation."

I thanked Andrew for his cooperation and bid him farewell, promising to keep him informed of any developments. As I left the office and returned to my car, I dialed Kendall's number to update her on the conversation and the lead we had uncovered.

"Kendall, I just spoke with Andrew Kallaway, Joss's son," I began as she answered the call. "He mentioned tensions within Joss's Amway network, particularly with a distributor named Lisa Thompson. She resides in Mehlville. Let's add her to our list of people to investigate."

Kendall's voice crackled with excitement on the other end. "Great work, RD. I've also made some progress. I spoke with Joss's other child, Sarah, who lives in Kentucky. She had some interesting insights. Let's meet up and exchange information."

CHAPTER 16

The aroma of freshly brewed coffee enveloped the air as Kendall and I sat at a corner table in our favorite coffee shop. Our laptops and notes were spread out before us, a reflection of the progress we had made in our investigation into the murder of Joss Kallaway.

"I spoke with Lex, Joss's daughter in Kentucky," Kendall began, her voice brimming with excitement. "She mentioned that Joss had become increasingly frustrated with her Amway business. Apparently, there were disputes within the network, and Joss had clashed with a distributor named Lisa Thompson."

I leaned in closer, captivated by Kendall's findings. "That aligns with what Andrew, Joss's son, mentioned to me. Lisa Thompson resides in Mehlville. It seems she might hold the key to unraveling this web of connections."

Kendall nodded, her gaze focused. "Exactly. I've been digging deeper into Lisa Thompson's background. It turns out she has a history of conflict with fellow distributors. There have been allegations of deceptive practices and financial disputes. I've also discovered that she had a falling out with another distributor named Rachel Henderson a few months ago."

My curiosity piqued at the mention of Rachel Henderson. "Rachel Henderson? That's an interesting development. Do we know anything about Rachel's relationship with Joss? It might shed light on any potential motives."

Kendall furrowed her brows, deep in thought. "So far, I haven't found any direct connection between Rachel and Joss. But considering Lisa's falling out with Rachel and Joss's clashes with Lisa, there could be a link worth exploring. We should gather more information on Rachel's recent activities and any potential interactions she might have had with Joss or Lisa."

As we immersed ourselves in our investigation, the coffee shop buzzed with activity around us. We exchanged glances, knowing that the pieces of the puzzle were slowly falling into place.

CHAPTER 17

While I was heading home, feeling the weariness seep into my bones, I received a text message from Rachel, the good Rachel, as I liked to call her.

She asked if I wanted to grab drinks again that evening.

Despite my fatigue, I couldn't resist the opportunity to spend more time with her. After agreeing to meet Rachel, I headed home to change into something more appropriate for drinks at a bar downtown.

As I got ready, my mind continued to dwell on the case. The lack of progress frustrated me. It was disheartening to think that someone had gotten away with murder, and we didn't have any solid leads. The weight of the unresolved crime hung heavily upon me as I left my apartment and made my way to the designated meeting place.

When I arrived at the bar, Rachel was already there, looking stunning in a blue dress that complemented her blonde hair perfectly. Her smile brightened as she saw me, and we exchanged pleasantries before settling down and ordering our drinks. Rachel began to talk about her work as an

MLM distributor, and I listened with genuine interest.

"It's not an easy job, you know," she said, taking a sip of her martini. "There's a lot of pressure to constantly recruit new members and make sales. And it's not like a regular 9-to-5 job where you can leave work at the office. You're always thinking about ways to grow your business."

I nodded, taking a sip of my beer. "That sounds tough. Have you ever seen any shady practices in the industry?"

Rachel leaned in closer, her eyes filled with a mix of weariness and determination. "Oh, definitely. Some companies make unrealistic promises and pressure their members to buy large quantities of products that they'll never be able to sell. It's really sad to see some of these people lose so much money."

Her words resonated with me, and I couldn't help but think about the potential connection between Rachel's world and Joss's murder. I decided to inquire further, cautiously navigating the conversation. "Did you know Joss Kallaway? I heard she was involved in Amway as well."

Rachel's expression softened, and a hint of sadness flickered in her eyes. "Oh yeah! I knew her! It was sad to hear the news about her."

"How did you know her?" I asked, curiosity getting the better of me.

Rachel took a moment to gather her thoughts before responding. "She was my former upline in Amway. We worked closely together for some time before things took a turn."

The mention of Joss being Rachel's former upline piqued my interest. Could their relationship have played a role in the events leading up to Joss's murder? I decided to probe further. "Do you know anyone who worked with Joss in Amway, other than you?"

Rachel shook her head, her expression thoughtful. "No, I don't think so. But I do know that Joss was pretty high up in Amway. Maybe you should look into that. Sometimes success can draw unwanted attention."

Her words struck a chord within me, and I made a mental note to delve deeper into Joss's position within the Amway network. We finished our drinks and ordered some food, continuing to chat about our lives outside of work. The conversation flowed easily, and I found solace in the distraction it provided.

As we stepped out of the bar, the night sky greeted us with its clear expanse, adorned with twinkling stars. It was a beautiful sight, and for a brief moment, the weight of the case lifted, replaced by a sense of hope that justice would prevail for Joss and her grieving family.

"I had a great time tonight," Rachel said, her smile genuine and warm. "We should do this again sometime."

"I'd like that," I replied, returning her smile. "Thanks for the company."

We bid each other farewell and parted ways. Walking back to my apartment, I couldn't help but feel a glimmer of optimism flicker within me.

Part two

CHAPTER 18

As Kendall and I settled into the break room, seeking solace in the familiar routine of coffee and snacks, I couldn't help but notice the weariness etched on Kendall's face. Her eyes were heavy with exhaustion, a testament to the long hours we had spent tirelessly working on the case. She poured us each a cup of coffee, and I gratefully accepted the gesture, feeling the warmth seep into my tired bones.

"You okay?" I asked, concern lacing my voice, as I reached for a donut.

Kendall nodded, her eyes reflecting a mix of fatigue and frustration. "Just tired. And frustrated. It feels like we're hitting dead ends on both cases."

I could empathize with her sentiments. Despite our diligent efforts, interviews with potential witnesses and suspects had yielded little in terms of substantial leads. I took a sip of coffee, my mind racing for a way to uplift Kendall's spirits.

"You know," I began, pausing to collect my thoughts, "we might be approaching this from the wrong angle. Perhaps we're too focused on the MLM aspect, and we're overlooking other potential avenues."

Kendall's eyebrow raised in curiosity. "What do you mean?"

"Well, Joss's involvement in Amway could be a red herring. What if there are other aspects of her life that we haven't explored thoroughly? We should dig deeper into her personal connections, her relationships, and her financial situation. There might be hidden motives or unexpected connections we've missed."

Kendall's expression softened, and a glimmer of hope flickered in her eyes. "That's a valid point. Maybe we need to broaden our perspective. Let's start delving into Laura's personal life and see what we uncover."

A smile tugged at the corners of my lips. "See? We make a good team."

Kendall returned the smile, a hint of relief evident in her eyes. "Yeah, we do."

The weight of the case temporarily lifted as we finished our coffee and donuts, sharing a moment of respite amidst the chaos.

With renewed determination, we returned to our desks, ready to delve into Laura's life with a fresh perspective.

CHAPTER 19

I slumped onto the couch, the weight of the day's revelations pressing heavily upon me. Thoughts swirled in my mind as I tried to make sense of the tangled web of secrets and tragedies surrounding the case. The air in my living room felt heavy, suffused with a mixture of frustration, sadness, and determination.

Just as I was about to lose myself in the abyss of my thoughts, my phone rang, breaking the silence. I glanced at the screen and saw Rachel's name flashing across it. A sense of relief washed over me, grateful for the distraction and the opportunity to share the burden with someone who understood.

I answered the call, my voice laced with a mix of weariness and anticipation. "Hey, Rachel. It's good to hear your voice."

"Hey, RJ," Rachel replied, her voice tinged with concern. "You sound exhausted. Are you okay?"

I sighed, grateful for her perceptiveness. "Yeah, it's been a long day. We received some tough news from the captain. Laura was pregnant. It's heartbreaking, Rachel. Two lives lost, and we have to find the person responsible."

There was a brief pause on the other end of the line, followed by a soft sigh. "That's devastating, RJ. I can't even imagine what you're going through. How are you holding up?"

Her genuine concern was like a balm to my weary soul. "It's tough, Rachel. The weight of the case feels heavier now. But I'm determined to find justice for Laura and her unborn child. We owe them that."

"I know you're doing everything you can, RJ," Rachel reassured me, her voice filled with unwavering support. "Sometimes, these cases take unexpected turns, and it can be overwhelming. But don't forget to take care of yourself in the process."

Her words resonated deeply within me, a gentle reminder amidst the chaos. "You're right, Rachel. It's important to stay grounded and find moments of respite. Thank you for reminding me."

We continued to talk, exchanging stories and moments of vulnerability. Rachel's soothing presence provided a much-needed respite from the relentless pursuit of the truth. We delved into our personal lives, sharing our hopes, fears, and dreams outside the realm of our demanding jobs.

As the conversation flowed, Rachel's words sparked a newfound perspective within me. She shared her own experiences of facing adversity, offering valuable insights that helped me see the case from a different angle. Her wisdom and empathy acted as a beacon of light amidst the darkness that had enveloped my thoughts.

"I believe in you, RJ," Rachel said, her voice filled with unwavering conviction. "You have the strength and determination to navigate through this storm. Remember, you're not alone in this. I'm here for you."

Her words filled me with renewed vigor, rekindling the flickering flame of hope within my weary heart. The weight of the case seemed momentarily lighter as Rachel's unwavering support lifted my spirits.

"Thank you, Rachel," I said, my voice filled with gratitude. "Your presence in my life means more to me than words can express. I'm lucky to have you as a friend."

The conversation continued, stretching into the late hours of the night.

As we bid each other goodnight, a renewed sense of purpose and determination filled me.

CHAPTER 20

After the confrontation, I decided to take a break from the case and focus on clearing my head. I took the afternoon off and went for a long drive in my car, blasting some classic rock tunes and trying to forget about the stress of the investigation.

As I drove aimlessly, I couldn't help but think about Kendall's accusations. Was she right? Had I been too focused on one thing and not enough on the other leads? Something about it just didn't sit right with me, and I was determined to find out what.

Lost in thought, I didn't even notice when my phone rang.

It was Rachel.

I hesitated for a moment before answering, still feeling guilty about using her for information.

"Hey Rachel, what's up?" I said, trying to sound casual.

"I'm sorry to bother you, RJ, but I thought you might want to hear this," she said, her voice hushed.

"Go on," I said, suddenly interested.

"I overheard some of my Monat uplines talking about the murder case you're working on," she said, and my heart skipped a beat.

"What did they say?" I asked eagerly.

"They were discussing how the victim had been involved in several MLMs before joining Monat, and they seemed to think that might have something to do with her murder," Rachel said, her words tumbling out in a rush.

My mind raced as I tried to process this information. If the victim had been involved in multiple MLMs, that could explain why she was targeted.

Maybe someone was trying to silence her before she exposed something about the industry.

I thanked Rachel for her help and ended the call, feeling a renewed sense of purpose.

As I drove back to the precinct, I couldn't help but wonder what other secrets she was possibly hiding.

And more importantly, who was willing to kill to keep them hidden?

Chapter 21

In the bustling streets of Downtown St. Louis, the woman hurriedly made her way through the throng of pedestrians, her steps purposeful and determined.

She clutched her handbag tightly, the weight of anticipation hanging in the air around her. This evening marked another Amway meeting, a gathering she attended faithfully, drawn to the promise of success and financial freedom.

As she entered the building, the sound of lively chatter and the scent of excitement enveloped her. The room was abuzz with eager distributors, mingling and exchanging stories of triumph and ambition. The woman smiled, joining in the camaraderie, momentarily forgetting the mundanity of her everyday life.

The meeting progressed, filled with motivational speeches, success stories, and the allure of a brighter future. She listened attentively, captivated by the fervor of those around her. The promise of wealth and the possibility of breaking free from the constraints of her current circumstances were tantalizing.

As the evening drew to a close, a man approached her, his eyes twinkling with charm and confidence. He introduced himself as Mark, an experienced distributor with a charismatic aura that drew her in. Intrigued, she engaged in conversation with him, their words flowing effortlessly.

Mark's charisma and ambition were contagious, leaving her yearning for more. He invited her to join him for a drink, a chance to discuss strategies and potential partnerships. Eager to deepen her involvement in the Amway network, she accepted his invitation, her heart pounding with a mix of anticipation and curiosity.

They stepped into a nearby bar, the dimly lit atmosphere lending an air of intimacy to their conversation. As they shared their visions and aspirations, a magnetic pull grew between them. The allure of the night and the possibility of escaping their respective realities filled the air.

As the drinks flowed and inhibitions loosened, the subtle tension between them grew undeniable. In that moment, the boundaries of their professional connection blurred, giving way to an undeniable attraction.

The woman's mind raced with conflicting emotions, torn between the desire to explore this unexpected chemistry and the lingering caution of the choices she was about to make.

They left the bar, the night now cloaked in darkness and secrets. The woman's heart raced as she followed Mark to his apartment, a mixture of excitement and trepidation coursing through her veins. With each step, the weight of her actions became heavier, intermingled with a sense of liberation and an unspoken understanding of the temporary nature of their encounter.

Behind closed doors, inhibitions were shed, and their bodies intertwined in an intimate dance of desire. In that passionate embrace, they sought solace from their mundane lives, embracing the fleeting ecstasy of the present moment.

Hours passed, and the night eventually surrendered to the dawn. As the sun's first rays peeked through the curtains, casting a gentle glow upon their entangled bodies, the woman's thoughts turned introspective.

CHAPTER 22

The moon cast a pale glow through the window, bathing the bedroom in an ethereal light.

She slowly emerged from a restless slumber, her senses gradually awakening to the disorienting darkness that enveloped the room.

Uncertainty clouded her thoughts as she reached out, her fingers seeking solace in the familiar touch of her purse.

They instinctively found the cool surface of her purse, nestled amidst the shadows.

Careful not to disturb the peaceful slumber of her hookup, she slipped out of bed, her bare feet cautiously treading upon the worn floorboards.

Each step echoed softly in the stillness of the night as she made her way to the corner of the room, bathed in a dim glow from the moon's gentle rays.

With a flicker of hesitation, she unzipped her purse, the sound breaking the silence like a whispered secret. Her fingers sought out the small, metal object hidden within.

The weight of it pressed against her palm, a silent reminder of the choices she had made.

It was a pistol, its smooth surface cold against her skin.

Its significance bore down upon her conscience, mingling with the shadows of doubt and uncertainty that swirled within her mind.

In that solitary moment, the woman stood at the precipice of her own actions. The allure of the night, once enticing and thrilling, now carried a weight of regret.

She grappled with the consequences, torn between the darkness of her desires and the flickering light of morality that still lingered within her soul. Guilt and self-reflection cast a veil over her fragile state of mind, challenging her resolve.

Summoning her strength, she took a deep breath and retraced her steps back into the room.

The man stirred in his sleep, his voice a hazy murmur as he mumbled, "Where are you?"

The woman's heart skipped a beat, her grip on the pistol tightening involuntarily.

Her conflicted emotions swirled within her, but she knew she couldn't answer his inquiry.

She shot the man in the head multiple times. The loud sound of the bullet leaving the gun echoed throughout the room.

She quickly got on her dress, grabbed her purse, and left.

CHAPTER 23

I sat at my desk in the bustling police station, surrounded by the hum of activity and the faint scent of coffee wafting through the air. Papers and case files covered my workspace, evidence of the relentless pursuit of truth that defined my role as a detective.

It was just another day, or so I thought, until an anonymous call shattered the monotony.

The shrill ring of the phone sliced through the ambient noise, causing heads to turn and eyes to meet mine. I picked up the receiver, my curiosity piqued by the unknown caller on the other end. "Detective RJ Mitchell speaking," I announced, my voice steady and professional.

A soft, hesitant voice greeted me from the other end of the line. "Hello, Detective Kegan. I...I have some information about the recent murder case you're working on."

My heart quickened its pace, the sudden surge of adrenaline fueling my senses. "I'm listening," I replied, my tone eager yet cautious.

The caller hesitated for a moment before continuing, her voice trembling with a mixture of fear and determination. "Last night, I heard a loud bang coming from the neighboring house. I peeked through my curtains, and I saw a woman leaving the house and getting into her car. I managed to catch the license plate number."

My grip on the phone tightened, anticipation and curiosity intertwining within me. "Can you tell me the license plate number?" I asked, my voice betraying a mix of urgency and hope.

The caller recited the series of numbers and letters, each syllable resonating in my mind as I jotted them down. I felt a knot form in my stomach as the realization dawned upon me. I recognized those characters all too well; they belonged to none other than Rachel's vehicle.

"Thank you for sharing this information," I said, my voice filled with gratitude. "You've been incredibly helpful. Rest assured, we will investigate this immediately."

As the call ended, I sat back in my chair, my mind racing with a myriad of thoughts and emotions. I had known Rachel for some time now, and the possibility of her involvement in the case sent shockwaves through my core. But as a detective, I had a duty to pursue the truth, no matter how uncomfortable it may be.

I approached Kendall, my partner and confidante, sharing the details of the call with her. Her eyes widened, mirroring the gravity of the situation. We knew we had to act swiftly, to confront Rachel and seek answers that would either confirm or dispel our suspicions.

"We need to pay Rachel a visit," I said, my voice laced with determination. "We can't afford to ignore this lead."

Kendall nodded, her expression a mix of concern and resolve. "Let's gather our evidence and prepare ourselves for what we might uncover. We owe it to the victim, to Joss, and to the pursuit of justice."

Together, we meticulously organized our findings, double-checking every detail to ensure we had a solid case against Rachel. The weight of the truth rested heavily upon our shoulders, urging us onward in our pursuit.

As the sun dipped below the horizon, casting an amber glow over the city, Kendall and I found ourselves parked in front of Rachel's residence.

The air crackled with tension as we prepared to confront the woman who had unknowingly become a prime suspect in our investigation.

With a deep breath, I stepped out of the car, my gaze fixed on the door ahead. Shadows danced along the walls, an eerie reminder of the darkness that lurked within our pursuit of justice. We exchanged a nod, our unspoken bond reinforcing our shared commitment to uncovering the truth.

As we approached Rachel's front door, I couldn't help but wonder what secrets lay hidden behind its wooden facade. The night held its secrets close, but it was our duty to expose them, to unveil the shadows that obscured the truth. The path ahead was treacherous, but we were determined to navigate it, no matter the cost.

With a resolute knock on the door, we stood poised at the precipice of revelation.

CHAPTER 24

"Hey RJ, what brings you here?" Rachel greeted me with a warm smile.

"I wanted to ask you a few more questions about Laura's case if that's alright," I said, stepping into her house.

"Sure thing, let's sit down in the living room," Rachel said, leading me to the couch.

I took out my notebook and pen as we settled down. "What information do you know about this incident?"

Rachel looked at me with surprise. "What do you mean?"

"Well, Laura was pretty high up in Amway, and you used to be in her downline. I need to know what you have heard, what you know for a fact, and what you heard as rumors." I explained.

Rachel thought for a moment before responding. "I don't have that much information, to be honest."

"Tell me what you know about her other downline members."

"I don't know any of the people Laura was involved with, but I do know that there are some shady characters in her branch who will do anything to make a quick buck."

"Can you give me any names or specific instances of shady behavior?" I probed.

Rachel shook her head. "I'm sorry, RJ. I don't feel comfortable sharing that information. It's just rumors, anyways."

I could sense that she was holding something back, but I didn't want to push too hard. "Okay, I understand. Is there anything else you can tell me about Laura that might be relevant to the case?"

Rachel thought for a moment before responding. "Well, I do know that Laura used to have people over for Amway meetings quite often. But I never met any of them, so I can't give you any names."

"That's still helpful, thank you," I said, jotting down the information in my notebook.

As I got up to leave, Rachel walked me to the door. "I hope I was able to help in some way."

"You definitely did, Rachel. Thank you for your time," I said, giving her a small smile before heading out the door.

I has a gut feeling I was a step closer.

CHAPTER 25

As soon as I got into the office the next morning, I went straight to Kendall's desk.

She was already typing away on her computer, so I leaned over her shoulder to show her the text message from Rachel. "This is her," I said, pointing to the screen.

Kendall studied the message for a moment before nodding her head. "Okay, let's look her up and see what we can find." She pulled up her browser and began typing, quickly pulling up Rachel's social media profiles and any news articles that mentioned her name.

I peered over her shoulder, scanning the information we found. "She's a Monat distributor," I noted, pointing to a post on her Instagram page that advertised the hair care products.

Kendall raised an eyebrow. "Multi-level marketing, huh? Those companies can be pretty sketchy. I've heard some horror stories about people getting sucked into those schemes and losing everything."

I nodded in agreement. "Yeah, but it doesn't necessarily mean she's involved in the murder. We just need to talk to her and see what she knows."

Kendall stood up from her desk, grabbing her coat. "Let's go pay her a visit then."

We drove to Rachel's apartment, which was located in a modest complex on the outskirts of town. As we approached the door, I could feel my heart racing with anticipation. We didn't know what we were walking into, but we were determined to get some answers.

Rachel answered the door and welcomed us inside, offering us seats on her couch. I couldn't help but feel a bit uneasy as I looked around her apartment. It was cluttered with Monat products and marketing materials, and the air was thick with the scent of artificial fragrances.

Kendall got right to the point, asking Rachel about her connection to the murder victim. Rachel hesitated for a moment before admitting that she had met her at an Amway business briefing.

"Can you tell us anything else about that meeting?" Kendall pressed.

Rachel shook her head. "I'm sorry, but I didn't really talk to her that much. It was just a brief introduction."

I could tell that Kendall wasn't satisfied with that answer, so I decided to take a different approach. "So, how did you get involved with Monat?" I asked.

Rachel's face lit up as she launched into a passionate explanation of the company and its products. She told us about the bonuses and incentives that distributors could earn, and the sense of community and empowerment that came with being a part of the Monat family.

Kendall and I exchanged a knowing glance.

We had heard all of this before from other MLM distributors we had encountered in our investigations. It was clear that Rachel had been brainwashed by the company's propaganda.

As the conversation continued, I couldn't shake the feeling that Rachel was hiding something from us. She kept glancing nervously towards the window, as if she was expecting someone to come barging in at any moment.

Suddenly, she excused herself to go to the bathroom. Kendall and I exchanged another glance as we heard her footsteps retreating down the hall. I followed her movements on the security camera feed we had set up, and I watched in disbelief as she climbed out the bathroom window and into her car.

"Kendall, she's running!" I shouted, sprinting towards the door.

We burst outside just in time to see Rachel speeding away in her car, leaving us standing there in shock.

CHAPTER 26

Adrenaline courses through my veins as Kendall and I pursue Rachel's car. The thrill of a car chase is unfamiliar to me, and I pray that I don't lose control of the vehicle. We navigate through the congested traffic, sirens blaring, while Kendall frantically communicates with dispatch for backup. Time is of the essence; we must apprehend Rachel before she slips away once more.

As we make a sharp turn, Rachel's car comes into view, and I catch a glimpse of her in the driver's seat. Her face displays a mixture of fear and determination as she accelerates, determined to escape at all costs. We push our own vehicle to its limits, closing the gap, but just as we near her, she swerves abruptly, colliding with a parked car.

Kendall and I hastily exit our car, adrenaline still surging through our veins. With guns drawn, we sprint towards Rachel's disabled vehicle. She emerges from the wreckage, and we shout for her to surrender, demanding that she raise her hands.

"SLMPD! FREEZE! HANDS UP IN THE AIR!" Kendall shouts.

After a brief hesitation, she complies.

Working swiftly, we secure her with handcuffs and escort her to the backseat of our squad car. I can feel my heart pounding in my chest as we drive back to the station, the weight of the chase still hanging heavily in the air. Once we arrive, we lead Rachel directly to the interrogation room, knowing that the real battle has only just begun.

The interrogation room is dimly lit, casting elongated shadows on the walls. Rachel is seated at the metal table, her eyes filled with a mix of defiance and fear. Kendall and I take our places across from her, ready to delve into the depths of her motivations and the events that led to this tragic situation.

I break the silence, my voice firm yet empathetic. "Rachel, we need to understand why you did what you did. Help us fill in the missing pieces of this puzzle."

Rachel's eyes dart nervously between Kendall and me, and then start to become wet. "I don't know what you're talking about!" and starts to lightly cry.

"You won't understand," she mutters, her voice tinged with guilt.

Kendall leans forward, her voice calm but assertive. "Rachel, we're here to listen. We want to understand your perspective. Give us a chance to help you."

Rachel's gaze softens momentarily, a flicker of vulnerability crossing her face. "It wasn't fair," she begins, her voice laced with bitterness. "Laura was earning more than me when I was in her downline, rising the ranks left and right. I felt invisible, like my hard work meant nothing. I didn't want to resort to violence, but I thought it was the only way to level the playing field."

I exchange a glance with Kendall, both of us recognizing the toxic combination of envy and desperation that drove Rachel to such drastic measures.

"The other woman's sister kept harassing me when I left. She would stalk me, call me a quitter, and call me a terrible business owner. CONSTANTLY! I had no *choice!*"

I lean in closer, my voice filled with compassion. "Rachel, we understand that it was a difficult situation for you, but there are always other ways to address grievances. Taking a life is never the answer."

Rachel's eyes well up with tears, her voice trembling. "I know, I know. I never wanted it to come to this. I just couldn't see any other way out."

Kendall reaches across the table, her voice gentle but firm. "Rachel, it's important for you to understand the consequences of your actions. There are people whose lives have been shattered by this tragedy. We need your cooperation to bring some semblance of justice and closure to them."

Rachel's resolve wavers, her shoulders slumping. "What do you need me to do?"

We provide Rachel with an overview of the evidence against her and the potential avenues for cooperation. The conversation delves into intricate details, discussing timelines, relationships, and the events leading up to the crime. The room becomes a mosaic of intense emotions, ranging from anger and disappointment to glimpses of remorse and regret.

CHAPTER 27

Hours pass as we meticulously unravel the web of deception and violence, gradually piecing together the truth. The conversation ebbs and flows, moments of intense dialogue interspersed with silent contemplation. Rachel, once guarded and defiant, begins to open up, sharing crucial insights that shed light on the intricacies of the crime.

Throughout the course of the conversation, Kendall and I maintain a delicate balance of empathy and professionalism.

We acknowledge Rachel's pain while emphasizing the importance of accountability and justice.

It's a delicate dance, navigating the boundaries between compassion and the pursuit of truth.

As the interrogation draws to a close, Kendall and I exchange a weary but satisfied glance. We have made significant progress in unraveling the case, but there are still challenges ahead.

Rachel is then haled off to be fingerprinted and placed in confinement.

The station is a hive of activity, officers bustling around, each consumed by their respective duties.

Kendall and I find a quiet corner, the weight of the day pressing down on us. We engage in a candid conversation, discussing the intricacies of the case, the emotional toll it has taken on us, and the weight of responsibility that comes with our roles as law enforcement officers.

"I can't believe the depths some people are willing to sink," Kendall says, her voice tinged with a mix of frustration and compassion. "But we have to keep going, for Laura and for all the victims affected by this."

I nod in agreement, the weariness of the day etched across my face. "You're right, Kendall. We owe it to them to ensure justice is served."

Epilogue

After the adrenaline of the chase died down, Kendall and I were left with the tedious paperwork that comes with making an arrest. I filled out forms and took notes while Kendall typed away on the computer.

As we worked, Kendall asked me a question that caught me off guard.

"So, how did you and Rachel actually meet?" Kendall asked, pausing from her typing.

I hesitated for a moment, not wanting to revisit the memory of Rachel and the case. But I knew Kendall deserved an answer.

"Well, I actually approached her at a restaurant," I said, feeling a little embarrassed.

Kendall looked at me with surprise. "Really? That's bold."

I shrugged. "I guess I was feeling bold that day."

Kendall chuckled. "Maybe next time, you should try a dating app like Tinder. Might save you some trouble."

I laughed, feeling a little relieved that Kendall could joke about it now. "Yeah, maybe I should."

About the Author

Bestselling author Ian Schrauth, born and raised in St. Louis, Missouri, has been captivating readers since he began publishing in 2014. Currently attending St. Louis Community College, Ian is pursuing a degree in Computer Science while working as a staff writer for the college newspaper, *The Montage*. His distinct voice and groundbreaking themes have established him as one of the only authors in Anti-MLM (Anti Multi-Level Marketing) fiction, with titles such as *The Opportunity*, and *The American Way: The good, the bad, and the lies I've learned from being an Amway IBO*.

In addition to his writing, Ian owns HeartStone Virtual Solutions, where he combines his technical expertise with a passion for creative projects. Ian continues to live and write in St. Louis, Missouri.

https://links.ianschrauth.com
https://books.ianschrauth.com